Under the GOLDEN Rain Tree

Written By

Eileen Hobbs

Illustrated By

Carli Valentine

Under the GOLDEN Rain Tree

First edition May 2023

Jacket design by Virginia McKevitt

Manufactured in the United States of America
ISBN: 979-8-9875646-0-8 (paperback)
ISBN: 979-8-9875646-1-5 (hardback)

DEDICATION

To my siblings and the other MKs (missionary kids) and friends I grew up with in Thailand. May you find joy in reading this and remember your own special times in the Land of Smiles and Golden Temples.

ACKNOWLEDGMENTS

Thank you to Carli Valentine for the wonderful illustrations; to Amy Le and Quill Hawk Publishing for all their hard work and advice; and to Paige V. for being the best beta reader ever!

English word	Thai spelling	Pronunciation
a good person	เป็นคนดี	kohn dee mak
elephant	ช้าง	chang
fat/fatty	อ้วน	ooh en
father	พ่อ	pah
flower	ดอกไม้	dawk mai
friend	เพื่อน	puen
good heart	ใจดี	chai dee
go together	ไปด้วยกัน	by duey khan
guava	ฝรั่ง	farang
gold	ทอง	tong
sugar cane	อ้อย	oi
Thai greeting	ไหว้	wai
it doesn't matter	ไม่เป็นไร	mai pen rai
white	สีขาว	kow
jasmine	ดอกมะลิ	dawk mali
little	เล็ก	lek
mother	แม่	mah
ong	อ่อง	ong
pretty	สวย	soo-ee
rambutan	เงาะ	gnaw
Thai buffalo	ควาย	kwai
rattan ball	ตะกร้อ	takraw
thank you	ขอบคุณ	kawp-koon ka (girl)
		kawp-koon kop (boy

MAP OF THAILAND

TABLE OF CONTENTS

Chapter 1

THE VILLAGE

An emerald-colored beetle the size of a pecan buzzed and flew sidc to side into Lily's open window like a miniature plane landing on the runway. The runway, in this case, was her flowered bedspread. It crawled slowly towards her. She examined it closely, admiring its shiny green back. She reached out to touch it with her one good hand but just as she did, it sprung up and flew out the way it came. She followed it to the window, watching it disappear over the lime-green rice fields below her. Here and there, muddy gray water buffalos ducked their heads down to chew grass, swinging their tails back and forth lazily. It would rain soon, Lily thought, just as it did almost every day this time of year. It was monsoon season in Thailand, and she loved watching the rain clouds build up and then burst forth. It sounded like hundreds of miniature drummers clattering loudly on their tin roofs.

"Lily!" her mother called from the other room. "I need you to go to the village and get more supplies."

Lily frowned, not answering at first. She hated going to the village. Not the walk – the walk there was beautiful, down and around the mud path that wound away from their house, down the mountain, and into the small village about a mile away. But there in the village… that was where it all would start up again. The taunting. The name-calling. "Fork fingers" some would call her, or "no hand Lily." She looked down at her useless right hand. It was a stub at the end of her arm where a normal hand was supposed to be. Two flimsy fingers, like tiny scissors, hung lifelessly. Even though she had been born this way, she still felt ashamed when she looked at it.

"Lily," her mother called again, more in-sistent this time.

She sighed, hopped off her bed, and closed the mosquito netting back around. It was no use. She would have to go. This was one thing she could do to help her mother and sister. She could not do the beautiful needlework that they did – that took two healthy hands. Neither could she help her father in the rice fields. It would be too dangerous for her to work with just one hand.

She walked reluctantly into the next room where her mother and sister sat on a bright pink vinyl mat on the wooden floor. All around them were small plastic bins filled with tiny colorful beads. Without looking up, her mother poked a needle into several small beads and slid them onto a tiny wire. Her hands and fingers moved quickly and gracefully, forming long strands of vibrant colors. After several of these strands were formed, she would twist and braid them into beautiful turquoise, pink, and blue bracelets. The bracelets were taken to the headquarters in the village where the company owners would pack them up and send them off to various parts of the world. Lily sometimes wished she could be one of those bracelets and disappear to another place far from here. Maybe America? Maybe Europe? She had read about all those places in her schoolbooks. But they were just a dream. Her mother and sister worked very hard, several hours a day, to help make enough money for all of them.

"Take these with you," her mother said, handing her a paper bag of bracelets. "They need to go to The Rainbow House. Bring back plenty of supplies."

Her mother took some Thai money, five twenty Baht bills, from a small pouch next to her and gave it to Lily.

"Be back before dark please."

thai baht

"And stay out of trouble," her older sister Jasmine called after her. At twelve, Jasmine was just two years older than Lily, but she liked to boss Lily around. Lily guessed it made her feel important.

Lily grabbed her book bag and went to the open doorway of their house and climbed down the wooden stairs.

Their house, like many here, was built up on stilts to keep them safe from floods. She shooed a few chickens out of her way and patted one of their muddy pigs that she called

Oowen, which meant "fatty." Then she began the long trek to the village.

She loved this walk. On either side of her were rolling green hills. Just beyond their rice farm, there were several rows of bright golden-yellow chrysanthemum flowers. They were very popular flowers, used for making teas, and for decoration at festivals and celebrations. This color of gold represented the king, who was loved and respected by all Thais. Along-side the path grew various flowers and plants. Honeysuckle and jasmine flowers wound through the banana and papaya trees, their sweet perfume filling the air. She stepped over to a banana tree and picked three small, ripe bananas from it. It might make a good snack for later.

There were a few houses like hers along the way – made of wood, built up on stilts, with tin or thatched roofs. Frangipani trees with their white flowers and bright yellow centers bloomed cheerfully.

Here, on the path, Lily was happy. She stopped at a rickety wooden bridge and looked over the side. A pond covered in waxy green leaves spread out to either side. Here and there, pink lotus flowers sat atop the leaves, opening to the sky like a woman's beautiful long painted nails.

The bridge meant she was near the village now. She slowed down, glancing ahead nervously. She held her two-fingered hand close to her, protecting it from what was to come.

Lotus flower

At the edge of the village, several shops lined either side of the dirt road. Plastic chairs, umbrellas, shoes, and pots and pans spilled out of one store. Colorful children's clothes swung in the breeze in another. Reddish brown curry spices were piled high next to burlap bags full of white jasmine rice. The smell of open fires burning filled the air.

"Hey, small hand!"

Just ignore them, Lily thought, seeing the group of boys playing with a dusty soccer ball out of the corner of her eye. She knew them well. They were always the ones that teased her about her deformed hand.

"Lily! Show us your scary hand!" another boy yelled. They lifted their own hands in the air and shook them as if she were a ghost they wanted to scare away. They all laughed. Lily felt the tears sting her eyes. Do not cry. Do not cry, she told herself.

"You! Boys! Go now! Before I hit you with my broom!"

Lily turned to see Mrs. Boonsom yelling at the boys from in front of her store. She was sweeping the cement floor where her tables of yellow and green fruit were piled high. Her hair was silver and cropped short. She wore a white cotton top with a gold and black *pa-toong*, the typical Thai batik skirt. She grinned at Lily, showing the blackened teeth of a long-time beetle nut chewer.

"*Mai pen rai,*" Mrs. Boonsom said, which meant, "it doesn't matter" or "don't mind them." She smiled and waved for Lily to keep moving. Lily waved back with her left hand and ran through the village, away from the hurtful taunts of the boys. Every time, she thought. Would it ever stop?

She continued on, watching two girls play rubber band jump rope. She had played it before, but it was difficult to make the jump rope with just her left hand. She had tried so many times to write and work with her left hand, but it felt so clumsy, and no one could read her writing. For rubber band jump rope, you had to string together rubber bands until it was long enough to jump over. Two other girls were on the floor of their parents' shop playing a game called *met kep* or pick up rocks. It was like Jacks but with small pebbles. It was yet another game she couldn't play because you had to gather rocks in your palm, toss them in the air, and have them land on the top of your hand. She sighed, wishing for the hundredth time that she were left-handed or had two normal hands.

A few minutes later she climbed the steps up to a white cement building. Faded pink curtains stirred lightly in the open windows. She knocked softly at the bright blue, painted door.

Inside, the room looked very similar to her own house, except there were at least fifty containers filled with rainbow colors of beads. Several women and teenage girls in their colorful *patoongs* sat around the room, bent over their needlework. Cardboard boxes filled with bracelets that were to be sent off around the world were piled up in every corner. Soft laughter erupted occasionally as the women discussed the funny events of their lives.

"Hello, Lily." It was Sandra, the owner of

the Rainbow House bracelet company. She
was British. She spoke a little bit of Thai, and
Lily could speak some English.

"Hello," Lily murmured, bringing her good
hand and her two-fingered one up to her face
in the traditional *wai* or Thai greeting.

They all knew about her hand, but she still
felt self-conscious around others.

"I need more beads," Lily said softly, handing Sandra the bag full of completed bracelets.

Sandra opened the bag and examined each bracelet, smiling as she rubbed her fingers across the smooth beads. "I think your mother and sister made these extra beautiful. Very *sooey*," she said, using the Thai word for pretty. She smiled and handed Lily an envelope of cash and a box full of new, colored beads. "Thank you so much!"

Lily gave a half smile and turned to go. She stopped suddenly, noticing a pad of paper and paintbrushes on a low table near the door. She reached down and touched the soft tip of one of the brushes. There was a small rectangular metal box that held five squares of bright paint.

"Do you like to paint, Lily?" Sandra asked.

Lily shook her head. "No. I mean… I can't." She motioned to her limp hand.

"Go ahead and take these," Sandra said. "Give it a try with the other hand! We keep these here for the kids of the women who work here so they don't get too bored."

Lily looked longingly at the bright colors and the crisp white paper. "No…" she started. "I can't…" She turned away.

"Wait!" Sandra said. "Take this pad of paper, a brush, and a box of paints. If it doesn't work, then bring it back next time." Sandra put the items in a paper bag and handed them to Lily.

"Okay," Lily said quietly, sliding the package into her book bag. What was she thinking? There was no way she could paint a picture with just one hand. But she took the bag anyway. She didn't want to hurt Sandra's feelings by saying no to the gift.

She said thank you in Thai - *kawp khun ka* - and waved goodbye. As she left the Rainbow House, dark clouds formed over her head. She would have to run to beat the afternoon storm.

She felt more lighthearted now, thinking of the paints and paper Sandra had let her borrow. Maybe, she thought, maybe she could paint a picture. Wouldn't her parents be so proud if she could make something beautiful?

A loud rumble and clap of thunder boomed over her head. She ran quickly through the village.

Chapter 2

THE STORM

At the edge of the village, the sky opened and pounded Lily with huge droplets of water. Should she keep going or find someplace to wait out the storm?

She decided to stop and take shelter under a blue and white striped awning at one of the stores. The wind whipped at the plastic above her like a helpless kite. The rain swept right at her, soaking her thin top and shorts. She held her book bag close to her, protecting it from the rain.

"You!" she heard behind her suddenly. She turned to see one of the mean soccer boys pointing at her, a scowl on his face. "What are you doing here? Go home!"

"It… it is pouring!" Lily stammered, suddenly afraid. The boys always said she was contagious. They were afraid their arms and legs would begin to transform into stumps if she was too close.

"Get away!" he yelled, raising the handle of a broom at her.

Lily glanced out into the torrent and back at the boy. She would take her chances in the rain, she thought, trembling with fear. Who knows what that crazy boy would do?

She darted out into the downpour. Immediately her whole body was soaked. She sprinted through the ankle-deep puddles, losing one of her flip-flops in the process. She shielded her eyes, looking for the path that led out of the village and up to the safety of her home in the mountains. She could not see one foot ahead of her.

Lily ran until she found herself under the shelter of a mango tree. Some of the yellow ripened fruit lay strewn around the base of the tree. She must have turned into the forest. She didn't know where she was, but at least she was protected from the pounding rain by the lush branches above her.

She continued until she came to the edge of a creek. The water had risen quickly, and it swirled and tumbled in front of her. There didn't seem to be a way across. "I'll just wait here under the trees until the rain stops," she thought. She started to turn away when the ground she was standing on gave way. Lily found herself sliding into the swollen, rushing water.

"Help!" The water pulled on her thin body. "I… can't… swim!" No one was there to hear her. The water carried her downstream. She splashed frantically, trying to keep her head above water. She tried to stand up and get a foothold but every time she felt the bed of the creek, a wave swirled around her and pushed her along the way. She felt a sharp pain on the side of her foot as she pushed off a jagged rock.

She wasn't sure how long she was carried this way but finally, the creek widened, and the water became calmer. She found her footing and half crawled out of the river, dragging her drenched body out onto the muddy banks. She lay there, breathing hard, her heart pounding. Blood flowed freely from the cut on her foot.

The rain stopped as quickly as it had begun. She opened her eyes and saw the glimmer of the sun as it began to slowly sink behind the blue mountains. It was getting dark and she didn't know where she was.

Lily sat up, slicking her short, wet hair back

from her face. She tried to stand up and winced from the pain in her foot. She looked for something familiar but there were only trees, vines, and rocks on either side of the creek. Amazingly, she still had her book bag slung across her shoulder.

She began to hobble along beside the creek. Surely, she would find a village or house nearby where she could ask for help? There was no one in sight and it was getting darker. She should find a place to rest for the night. Otherwise, she could get lost in the forest and never be found.

She spied a familiar tree with brilliant yellow flowers floating on its stems like small, lemon-colored tulips. She knew this tree. It had many names. The Royal tree, the Rain tree, but her favorite was the Golden Rain Tree. It was the national tree of her country.

Lily sat under the tree's spread of golden

blossoms. The setting sun lit the flowers on fire above her. She wiped away a tear. She had never been lost before. She had grown up near the forest but rarely ventured into it. She preferred the open air of the mountains near her house. She had no choice. She would have to wait until the morning before trying to find her way back.

Now that the sun was gone, she began to shiver from the cool night air. She pulled out the pad of paper, opened the paints, and laid them next to her. Hopefully, they would dry, and she would be able to still use them.

She took out the bananas from her bag and ate one hungrily. She set the other one next to her paints in case she needed it in the morning. It had been such a long day. She pulled her knees up close to her to stay warm and to make herself smaller. Who knew what beasts roamed around out here at night? Tigers? Wild boars?

She was scared and her foot hurt so much. She was surprised, then, that her weary eyes closed, and she fell asleep.

Chapter 3

RAMBU

Lily woke with a start, not sure where she was. Something had woken her – a rustling sound nearby. Or was it a snort? She wasn't sure. Then she remembered where she was. The sun was beginning to peek out. She breathed a sigh of relief. Surely, she could find her way home now.

She sat up, examining the large cut on her foot. It had stopped bleeding, but she wasn't sure she could walk on it. She looked around for her bag and paints. They had been spread out on the ground next to her. And something else. The paintbrush was next to the paper, but the paper was no longer white. Beautiful blue and red colors streaked across it. And her banana was gone.

"How…. what…" she said aloud. There was no one around. Had a ghost painted the picture? Then she saw round footprints leading away from the painting. They did not look human, but she did not know what type of mystical creature had come in the night and painted her a picture.

She tried to stand up on her wounded foot. "Ouch!" How could she walk on it? Suddenly she heard the rustling sound again. If it was a wild animal, maybe she should climb up the tree? Was it a tiger?

Her heart raced. She reached up for the first branch of the tree, ready to pull herself up to safety. Then the strangest thing appeared out of the bushes. It was a long, pinkish-white arm of some kind. It looked like the end of her own arm.

"What?" Before she could climb up, a head, attached to the snake-like arm, emerged. It was a huge head with enormous ears. On top of its head was a mound of wiry, white hair. Lily froze. The creature straightened out its snout and pointed it at her, making a noise like a rusty trumpet.

"Honk!"

Lily had seen elephants before, but she had never seen one like this. He looked like all the gray color had drained from his body. All that was left was a strange pink color, dotted with black freckles. Was she dreaming? Was it a white elephant? She had read about them! White elephants were extremely rare and were thought to have magical powers. She found that she was holding her breath. This was a baby about the same height as Lily herself. Was there a fierce mother elephant some-where?

The baby elephant stepped out of the bushes and walked cautiously toward her, its snout reaching out to sniff at her. She froze, feeling its hot breath on her. He had beautiful pale gray eyes and his eyelashes, the color of wheat, were long and fluttery. His snout settled on her bag, trying to open the flap.

"Are you hungry?" she asked softly, still afraid to move. Slowly, she reached into her bag and pulled out the last banana. The creature took it in its snout and then curled it around to put it into its mouth, swallowing it in one gulp. The snout came back to the bag, looking for more.

"I'm sorry friend," Lily said, patting him on his leathery head. "I'm all out!"

He made his honking sound again, startling Lily. She backed away. He stepped toward her. She backed away again. Finally, she stood still.

He used his snout to sniff her hair, and her bag and then, gently, sniffed at her two-fingered hand. It was a light touch, not meant to hurt her. He was curious. He touched her gently like a blind man might touch someone to know what they looked like.

Lily reached out to touch the wiry ball of hair on top of his head. She giggled! "It's like a rambutan," she said, referring to the egg-shaped, red, hairy fruit that she loved to eat. "Maybe I'll call you Rambu!"

The elephant opened her bag with his snout and pulled out the paintbrush. He gripped it in his snout and waved it back and forth.

"You!" Lily exclaimed. "You painted the picture!"

She watched in amazement as Rambu dipped the brush in the sticky paint and swiped back and forth on the paper.

"That's amazing! How do you do that?"

She studied him carefully. And then she had an idea. She took out another paintbrush and carefully put it in between the two nubs on her right hand. She watched Rambu use the top lip of his snout to curve around the paintbrush. She could do that too! One finger was longer than the other! She could curl it around the brush as Rambu did.

She sat next to Rambu, dipping into the paint, and laying out smooth strokes onto a fresh white paper. Rambu nodded his head up and down, stepping from side to side.

Lily wasn't sure how long they were there together, painting, but she finally heard a faint voice in the distance.

"Lily! Where are you?"

Someone was looking for her.

"I've got to go, Rambu! I'll try to come back. Okay? With more bananas!"

She limped toward the sound of the voices.

"Here!" she yelled back. "I'm here!"

She turned to take one more look at her artist friend, but Rambu was nowhere to be seen. Had it been a dream, she wondered? Was he real? She hoped so. She longed to see her new friend again.

Chapter 4

FOUND

It took another half an hour for Lily to meet up with her father and sister. Lily followed their voices and called out to them. Finally, through the brush, she saw them, and she half limped, and half ran into her father's wiry, muscular arms.

"What happened? Are you alright?" Lily's father looked down at her foot and saw the cut. "Here," he said, turning his back to her and kneeling so she could climb up for a piggyback ride.

Jasmine frowned at Lily. "Did you run away?"

Lily wasn't sure if she detected a bit of glee

or hopefulness in her sister's voice. "Of course not!" she exclaimed. "I got lost!"

As they tramped through the forest, Lily told them about the mean boys, the rainstorm, and losing her way. She didn't tell them about Rambu. That would be her secret. What if her dad told her not to go back and find Rambu again? What if bad men went into the forest searching for the sacred white elephant? They would want to capture him. He would be worth a lot of money.

As they walked, Lily reached into her bag and pulled out a handful of beads from Sandra's shop. Every few feet, she sprinkled a few of the colorful bits along the forest floor, like confetti. This would help her find her way back to Rambu.

When they got home, Lily's mother was pacing back and forth on the rough, wooden floor.

"Lily!" she exclaimed, folding Lily's small frame into her arms. Her mother said nothing for a moment, just held her.

It felt so good to be wrapped in her arms, Lily thought. Her mother rarely hugged her. Lily always thought she had been a disappointment to her because of her arm. But now, feeling her mother's warm embrace, those thoughts left her mind.

"I'm ok *Mah*," she said, using the Thai word for mother. While her mother washed and bandaged Lily's foot, Lily told her what had happened. When she came to the part about the boys, her mother stopped and looked at her.

"I am going to talk to their parents!" she said. "They should stay away from you. You are not normal like them! They should take pity on you!"

Her words cut Lily deeply. Not normal?

Not as good as other children? Tears stung her eyes. She pulled her bandaged foot away from her mother.

"I... am... normal!" she thought to herself, limping off to her room. She sat on her bed and emptied her book bag. She smoothed her hand across Rambu's painting. She limped to the bathroom and filled a pink plastic cup from the *ong*, a large ceramic barrel that kept their bathing water. She picked out a clean white sheet of paper and sat at her small wooden desk. How did Rambu grab the paintbrush again? She tried to remember. Slowly, she used the two pincers on her right hand to grasp the brush. She chose blue first and waved the brush back and forth on the paper to represent the sky. It felt so funny and awkward between her fingers. She kept on going. She rinsed her brush and then put bright spots of yellow on the paper. Under that, she used brown to make a vertical line. Finally, she used a mix of black and white to form a shade of gray and outlined the long snout and floppy ears onto Rambu's body. Her fingers cramped up, so she stopped, lifting the picture out in front of her. It wasn't bad, she thought. Was it? She had painted the blue sky and the bright yellow Golden Rain Tree. When her foot was better, she would take the picture and show it to Ms. Sandra. Even if it was ugly, Ms. Sandra would say something nice to her, she was sure of it.

She put the paper and paints away inside the drawer of her desk and clicked the lamp off. She heard the rumble of thunder and decided to close the wooden shutters of her window. She lifted the fine, lightweight cloth of her mosquito net and crawled into her bed. How comfortable it was compared to the floor of the forest, she thought. It was nice to be home.

Chapter 5

JASMINE

Lily's mother woke her early and brought her a steaming bowl of rice soup. Lily understood that this was her mother's way of apologizing for upsetting her the night before. She accepted it gratefully.

"Lily," her mother began hesitantly, examining the wound on Lily's foot, "the beads... did some of them spill out? There seem to be less in the bag this time."

Lily couldn't meet her mom's eyes. She stared down into her bowl and nodded. "In the water..." she said quietly. "I think they spilled out... I'm not really sure."

Her mother nodded as well. "Okay then. But next time, please be more careful."

Her mother left, leaving Lily feeling awful. What had she been thinking? The beads were so important to their family. Without them, fewer bracelets were made, and less money came in. She would have to find a way to make it up to her mom.

As she finished her rice, her sister Jasmine wandered into her room, a smug smile on her pretty face. Jasmine was a little taller than Lily and wore her hair longer, just passed her shoulder blades. Today she had it tied back in a braid. They were opposites in many ways. Jasmine liked to wear pretty clothes and ribbons in her hair. Lily didn't care about clothes. She just wanted to be outside and play or just sit and read a book.

"Well, "Jasmine said knowingly, "I hear you lost some beads?"

Lily stayed silent, eyeing her sister suspiciously.

"I think I know what happened to them!"
her sister went on.

Again, Lily said nothing, but her heart
pounded. Had her sister found out?

"I saw you!" she said suddenly, pointing at
Lily accusingly. "I saw you spilling them from
the bag. Why did you do that?"

Lily bent her head. What could she tell
Jasmine to keep her quiet? The truth? About
Rambu? She would think Lily was crazy. But
she didn't have a choice.

"Ok," she said finally, "but you have to
promise not to tell."

Jasmine eyed her younger sister through
squinted eyes. "We'll see. It depends on the
story."

Lily sighed and told her sister about the
beautiful white elephant she had seen and how

the elephant painted a picture for her. When Lily finished, Jasmine let out a single "Ha!" and then said, "You're lying. I'm telling mom."

"Wait!" Lily said, reaching out to grab her sister's arm. "I'll show you!" She reached into her desk drawer and pulled out the paintings Rambu had done and the one she had created of Rambu.

Jasmine studied them carefully. "This looks like a two-year-old painted this," she said finally, tossing the pictures on the bed. "This proves nothing!"

"I painted that one!" Lily said firmly.

Jasmine looked at her sister with a smirk. "There's no way you can paint with that broken hand." Lily cringed hearing the word "broken." It was even worse than what her mother said. "I'll tell you what. You do some of my chores for the next week and I'll keep your secret. Feed the chickens and pigs and wash the dishes."

Lily gave up and nodded. Again, she had no choice. Her sister didn't believe her. One day, she thought to herself, one day Jasmine would regret not believing her.

Chapter 6

THE PAINTINGS

Two days later, Lily's foot had healed enough to finally walk into town. She couldn't wait to show Sandra her picture and maybe even follow the beads to find Rambu again.

"You must come straight home!" her mother warned her. "Do NOT go into the forest again!"

Lily nodded, wondering how she could sneak into the forest without her mother knowing. Her mother seemed to have special powers of guessing where she had been.

Somehow, she didn't know why, but she felt more confident going into town. She didn't feel so afraid of the mean boys. She breathed in the air, which smelled like rain. It was September, still monsoon season, which meant it rained every day. Her mother had made her carry a plastic bag to cover herself in case of rain.

Today, instead of bananas, she stepped away from the path and scampered up a guava tree. The peel was lime green, but the fruit felt soft, so she picked two and put them in her bag. Maybe Rambu liked guava, she thought.

When she reached the edge of the village, the boys were nowhere in sight. Perhaps they were completing their chores. Lily breathed a sigh of relief and quickly ran down the dusty street. She climbed up the stairs to The Rainbow House.

"Hello!" Sandra called out when she saw Lily. Today Sandra wore a white cotton shirt and a knee-length blue cotton skirt. Her blonde hair was tied up in a loose ponytail. She was barefoot because it was customary not to wear shoes in the house. It was a sign of respect. Most houses had several pairs of shoes lined up at the front door. Lily removed her flip-flops and put her palms together in front of her face in the traditional Thai greeting.

Lily handed Sandra a bag of completed bracelets and waited for more beads and cash to take back to her mother. Should she show Sandra her painting, Lily wondered. She was suddenly afraid that Sandra would not like it. She turned to go but Sandra put a hand on her shoulder.

"Lily, did you try painting?" She made a motion with her hand like she was waving a brush on paper.

Lily nodded shyly.

"Show me!"

Lily slowly removed her artwork and laid

them on the table next to containers of blue and turquoise beads. She didn't show Ms. Sandra Rambu's painting. She wanted to keep it for herself.

Sandra didn't say anything for a moment as she examined each picture. Then she smiled at Lily.

"Lily, these are beautiful! May I keep them? I'll put them up on the walls here."

Lily didn't know what to say. Sandra liked her paintings! She could only nod happily. Sandra turned to put the pictures on the walls with some scotch tape. She couldn't believe that Sandra liked her artwork!

After leaving the Rainbow House, Lily ran to the edge of the village, but this time the boys were outside playing *trakaw*, a game with a small rattan ball. They stood in a circle, kicking the ball to each other off the inside of their ankles. They stopped in mid-play and stood in front of her. Lily trembled. They were all taller than she was. They were also barefoot and their feet were covered in dried red mud from playing in the street.

"Where are you going?" the oldest one asked, his arms on his hips. His nickname, *Lek*, meant "little" in her language, but he wasn't small. He was at least a foot taller than her.

Lily said nothing. She turned to go around him and another boy, Noi, stepped in front of her.

"You didn't answer the question, two-fingers," he said.

She made herself look at him. He had the traditional buzz cut, and his dark eyes gleamed with mischief. Lily took a deep breath. "I am doing something for Ms. Sandra," she said. "I have to get something and take it back to her."

The boys hesitated and looked at each other, not sure if Lily was telling the truth. But suddenly, as if by magic, they heard Ms. Sandra's voice behind them.

"Everything okay?" Ms. Sandra called. She was on her small blue scooter at a store just down from Lily and the boys. Lily couldn't believe her luck.

The boys stepped aside and let her pass. She breathed a sigh of relief and began to jog toward the edge of the forest. Thank you, Ms. Sandra, Lily thought. *Maybe my luck is turning around.*

Chapter 7

THE GIFT

Lily dashed into the forest, looking around for the huge mango tree. This was where they came out the day her father found her. She went around and around the roots of the tree, looking for some sign of the colored beads. Finally, she caught sight of three sparkling beads and walked in their direction. A few feet later, she found a few more and then another cluster of them. She continued this way, pushing leaves out of her way until she came into a small clearing. She could hear the bubbling of the small creek that had swept her downstream. She followed the stream until she saw the bright golden droplets of the rain tree rising above the forest. She ran towards it, looking around for more of Rambu's footsteps, but the rains had washed them away.

"Rambu!" she called, but all was quiet except for a warm breeze that rustled through the leaves above her. Should she wait? Should she try to find him?

She decided to sit down and wait for a while. She took out one of the guavas and bit into it. The sweet and tangy juice dribbled down her chin. Then she took out a piece of paper from her pad and laid out her paints and brushes. She stretched out on her stomach, grasped a brush between the two fingers on her right hand, and dipped it in the cup of water, then into the bright blue paint. With the blue, she made two bright mounds to look like the mountains around her village. Next, she picked the bright green paint and made tiny dots across the page. This would be the rice fields. Then her two fingers began to hurt.

Lily sat up and looked around. Did she hear something? She stood up.

"Rambu? I have a *farang* for you!" she said. She held out the oval-shaped guava in her left hand trying to lure Rambu towards her. Suddenly, she felt hot breath on her neck, and a pink snake-like snout reached out from behind her and snatched the fruit from her hand.

"Hey!" she said, spinning around. Then she laughed. She was face to face with the beautiful Rambu. Without thinking, she reached out to hug him and rubbed her hand across the stiff white hair on top of his head. He continued to chew the guava and then sniffed at her book bag for more food. She opened her bag for him to search with his long snout, and he found the other guava, sucked it up, and stuffed it in his mouth. Lily giggled.

"You're so silly!" She rubbed his rough, pink skin, and smoothed her hand over his floppy ears. As she studied him, Rambu was also studying her. His snout sniffed her hair, her two-fingered hand, and gently touched her face. A burst of happiness welled up inside her. She had never felt so loved.

Rambu reached his snout up into the Golden Rain Tree and plucked a cluster of bright yellow flowers. He handed it to Lily, and she knew that she had never received such a precious gift. He nudged her with his bulky body and curled his snout around her waist, tugging at her playfully. He pulled her closer to him and she realized he wanted her to climb on his back. She was afraid because he was still a baby, but she carefully put a leg over his back and slid on. Rambu began to trot, and Lily laughed, bumping up and down. He headed for the stream. When he got there, he dipped his long nose down into the water, then curled it backward and squirted Lily with a fresh spray.

"Hey!" she shrieked. She jumped off his back and splashed into the stream which was only up to her ankles today. She cupped the cool water in her hands and began splashing Rambu. He stepped into the stream with her, and she rubbed his rough, pink skin with water and sand from the bottom of the stream.

Suddenly a thunderous noise rang out from deeper in the forest. Both stopped playing to listen. Rambu's floppy ears perked up and he opened his mouth to let out a similar noise as if answering the call.

Lily stepped out of the stream, suddenly afraid. She knew what the sound was. It was a larger, full-grown elephant. She guessed it was Rambu's mother.

The loud sound rang out again, echoing throughout the trees. This time it was closer.

Lily's heart was beating so fast. She slowly backed up. The problem was that every time she took a step back, Rambu would take a step toward her.

"No Rambu!" she said, waving at him. "Go

find your mom. Go on!"

But it was no use. Rambu would not leave her.

Lily eyed a nearby tamarind tree, its hard-shelled brown fruit dangling from its leaves. She went towards it, finding a foothold and swinging up to the first branch, then the second. She looked down. Rambu stood looking up at her curiously. Then she heard a loud crash as Rambu's mother broke through the brush and rushed to Rambu's side, curling her long trunk around him protectively. She was enormous! The top of her head nearly touched the branch Lily stood on. Strangely, she wasn't white but the traditional gray of most elephants. She stood between Rambu and the tree and nudged him forward. They walked off together then, disappearing into the deep thicket of the forest.

Lily breathed a sigh of relief. She had no

idea what the mother elephant would do to her if she felt threatened. She sat for a moment longer, trying to calm her rapid breathing. Then she slowly slid down out of the tree.

She returned to the Golden Rain Tree to pick up her book bag. Next to it was the branch of bright yellow flowers Rambu had given her. She picked them up gingerly and placed them in her book bag, smiling. This day, she thought, had been the loveliest of days.

Chapter 8

THE MAHOUT

From that day on, Lily went to see Rambu whenever she could. And each time she visited him, he always left her a gift. She didn't know how or where he got them – did he have magic powers? – but she was so delighted to have them. One day, he left several bright pink lotus flowers in a circle around the Golden Rain Tree. Lily gathered them up in her arms and gave Rambu a big kiss on his head. He curled his trunk around her in a sweet hug. She carried the flowers back home and divided them in half, giving a bundle to her mother and one to Jasmine. At first, her mother frowned.

"Where did you get these?" She wondered if Lily had used some of the bracelet money to buy them.

"I picked them," she said, "in a pond down by the village!" Jasmine eyed her suspiciously but did not say anything.

One day, Rambu nudged Lily's hand, and she held it out to him. He placed a clam shell in it. She gently pried it open and inside sat a perfect, lustrous pearl.

"Rambu!" she cried out. "Where did you get this? You're not stealing from people, are you?" She giggled, thinking of Rambu using his trunk to sneak into people's windows.

As if he understood her, he shook his head back and forth, his soft pink ears fluttering. She patted his head and gave him another banana for a treat.

Every gift he gave her, she placed carefully into a wooden cedar box in the drawer of her desk. One day it was a bright blue hair ribbon that he waved back and forth in his trunk before he gave it to her. Another day it was a stone the color of amethyst. Another time it was a ruby red gemstone and then a dark green stone the color of the beetles that flew into her room. She had no idea where he was getting all these beautiful stones, but she placed each one carefully into her cedar box.

Some days he was waiting for her when she arrived. On other days, she would get her paints out and wait for him to come bursting through the nearby brush, honking at her. Then they would paint together – bright streaks of orange, blue, and purple.

She studied how he used his trunk to grasp the paintbrush and imitated his strokes with her two-fingered hand.

The women at The Rainbow House noticed the paintings and wondered who was making

the pictures of the mountains and elephants. But Lily had asked Sandra not to tell anyone who had painted them.

After a few weeks of bringing in her artwork, Sandra had a surprise for her. "Lily, you like to draw *chang* don't you?" she asked, using the Thai word for elephant.

Lily hesitated. Should she tell Sandra about Rambu? She decided against it. "I just like them," she said quietly.

Sandra sat down on a metal stool and motioned for Lily to sit next to her. "You know, there is someone in the next village who knows a lot about white elephants."

Lily's eyes grew wide. "You mean... he's seen them?" she asked.

"Not only has he seen them, he's worked with them. At the king's palace. He worked there for many years taking care of the white elephants owned by the king."

How could that be, Lily wondered. And how could she not have heard about this person? She had heard stories of the king owning white elephants, but she thought it was only a legend. "Who is it?" she asked.

"His name is Loong Kow." *Loong*, in Thai, meant uncle which was a respectful title for an elder. *Kow* meant white. Maybe it was from working with white elephants?

"He lives at the opposite end of the next village, about two miles up into the hills," Sandra continued. "He lives a very quiet life. He doesn't like many visitors. But he is very old and wise and is well respected."

Someone like that, Lily thought, would surely not want to see a girl with a deformed hand like hers. She smiled.

"Thank you for telling me." Lily rose to go.

"Would you like to meet him?" Sandra asked. "*By duey kan*," she said in Thai, meaning "We could go together."

Lily stared at Sandra in amazement. "Yes!" she said, unable to find the English words to say, "I can't believe it!"

When Lily left the Rainbow House, she felt as though she was dancing on air. She couldn't believe that tomorrow she would be going with Ms. Sandra to see Loong Kow and find out more about white elephants like Rambu.

Sandra sent Lily home with a note for her mom, asking permission to take Lily on a small trip. It was in English so Lily had to translate for her. Would her mother let her go? She hoped with all her heart she would.

Chapter 9

THE GIRL WITH THE
GOLDEN RINGS

Lily translated the note from Ms. Sandra to her mother.

"I don't understand," her mother said. "Why does she need you to go with her?"

Lily shrugged. "She just thought it would be a nice adventure for me."

Jasmine glared at her. "You haven't had enough adventures?" She turned to their mother. "How come Lily gets to go do that when I have to stay here and work?"

"Hush!" Lily's mother waved her hand at Jasmine. She turned to Lily. "I suppose it's okay. Just this one time."

Lily's heart beat faster. She had never been to that village before. She couldn't help herself. She smiled a great big smile at her grumpy sister. Jasmine turned around, but not before she saw Lily stick her tongue out at her.

"*Mah!*" Jasmine wailed again. "Lily stuck her tongue out at me." But their mother had had enough of their arguing and held up a palm for them to stop.

The next morning Lily walked down to the village. Thankfully, Lek and his friends were not around. She half skipped to The Rainbow House to meet Ms. Sandra, who was waiting for her outside. She motioned for Lily to get on the back of her scooter and fastened a black child's helmet around her head.

Lily felt like a bird flying as she rode on the scooter up the mountain. She wanted to put her arms out, but Ms. Sandra told Lily to hang on tight to her waist. They wove back and forth over a bumpy dirt road for several minutes before they saw a cluster of houses, like her own, up on stilts with thatched and tin roofs. A few stray black and brown dogs wandered across their paths, their tails wagging lazily. Papaya trees, with orange and green oblong fruit, lined the road.

Lily expected Loong Kow's house to be fancy. After all, he had worked at the King's palace. But it wasn't. It was smaller than her house. They climbed up the stairs and knocked on an rusty screen door.

Lily stared at the young girl who answered the door. She was beautiful, about Lily's age, but taller. What she wore around her neck startled Lily. Five thin brass rings wound around her neck, stretching it out and making her seem taller than she was. She wore a short purple and pink top and a black skirt. A bright red scarf covered her hair which had been wound up into a bun.

Lily stared, her mouth open wide. She heard about the "long neck" women of the Kayan Hill Tribe before, but she never met any of them. The girl put her palms together and bowed her head slightly to greet them.

Tong

Sandra turned to Lily and said, "This is Tong," which meant "gold" in English. "Loong Kow is her great-grandfather. Tong speaks English well, so I asked her to help translate for us."

Lily hid her two-fingered hand behind her back as they stepped inside and took off their shoes. The room was dimly lit and had very little furniture. She saw a teak desk to one side of the room and caught sight of two pictures above it. One picture was expected. It was of the King of Thailand in a bright golden uniform. Every house she had ever been in, including her own, had a similar picture. The other one was a faded photograph of a young boy riding atop a white elephant. The elephant was decorated with a gold cloth on its back, and it had a giant lei made of white flowers and pink ribbon draped around its neck.

In the middle of the room, she could make

out the shape of a very old man sitting cross-legged in the middle of the floor. A low wooden table sat in front of him. He was dressed simply in navy blue pants and a shirt, and he had scraggly white hair and a long white beard. He held a long silver pipe in his mouth, the smoke from it curling up and around his head like a ghost. But his eyes were the most fascinating part about him. They were milky white. "He's blind," Lily thought sadly. For once, she was not worried about what someone thought of her misshapen hand.

They sat on the floor in front of the old man, their legs tucked to their sides. Tong made the introductions. As she did, her grandfather put his pipe down and held out his hands to first Sandra and then to Lily. Lily gave him her left hand only and the old man cocked his head to the side.

"Where is your other hand?" he asked.

Slowly, Lily took her two-fingered hand out from behind her back and placed it in Loong Kow's brown leathery one. He gently touched the two limp fingers and smiled.

"My hand is... broken," Lily whispered, ashamed. Why did she use her sister's words to describe her hand?

"That's an odd phrase," Loong Kow said. "Do you think my eyes are broken?"

Lily wasn't sure what to say. He was blind, wasn't he? Didn't that make him broken?

"I just see differently," he finally said. "With my memories and my other senses."

"That's true!" Tong said. "He can hear the *chinchuks* crawling on the ceiling or a guava drop from a tree a mile away!"

Loong chuckled at his great-granddaughter's reference to the small house lizards. "Well, maybe not quite like that. But I can smell the rain a day before it comes. I can taste any spice or herb and tell you what it is. And I can feel with my hands…" He gently patted her two fingers. "And what I see here, young one, is not broken. It is just different."

He released her hand, and Lily cradled it to her. They were both silent for a moment. Could it be, Lily wondered, that she wasn't broken after all? That she, like Loong Kow, was just different?

"I have other senses too," Loong Kow continued. "And I sense that you have a secret, a very special secret. Some secrets are worth protecting."

Tong handed each of them a glass of sweet tea and then looked at Sandra expectantly.

"You have questions for Loong Kow?" she said.

Sandra nodded. "Yes. We would like to hear about his time at the palace taking care of the white elephants."

Tong translated and the old man nodded. "Why?" he asked, and Lily felt as though he were looking directly at her or even through her. She knew he wanted her to answer.

"I'm… I'm curious" she stammered.

"Very well," he said. "And after I tell you, then perhaps you will tell me the real reason?"

This startled Lily. Did he know she had met Rambu? And if so, how could he know?

Loong Kow began his story in a soft, mesmerizing tone. Tong translated for Sandra, her voice equally soft and melodic as if she were reading a poem.

"I was ten years old when I went to the palace to train to be a mahout." Lily knew that mahout meant someone who worked with and cared for elephants. Loong Kow continued. "My father was already there, and he sent for me. My father and his brother had discovered a white elephant not far from here and as is customary, when you find a white elephant, it is your job to offer it to the king. In return, the king allowed my father and uncle to stay at the palace and take care of their elephant. The elephant's name was The Silver One of the Precious Northern Village. But we called him just *Oi* – sugar cane – because he had such a good and sweet heart. And," he chuckled slightly, "sugar cane was his favorite food!" Uncle smiled and Sandra and Lily laughed quietly. It was clear that he had a close bond with his elephant.

"Why are white elephants so sacred?" Sandra asked.

Uncle nodded as if expecting this question. "First, they are very rare. Kings for many hundreds of years have ridden them. They believed they are very magical and spiritual beings. A white elephant, when discovered, shows the greatness of the king. They represent power, purity, and peace. A king with many white elephants will be successful. He will have a prosperous kingdom and he will reign for a long time. Just like our king now. If his elephants die, it means his kingdom is not strong."

They all sat quietly for a moment, thinking of the special bond that Loong Kow had with his beautiful elephant. Then he motioned to Tong, who rose and went to his teak desk. She opened a drawer and returned with a rusted metal box with a picture of an elephant on the front. She opened it for her great-grandfather.

"See?" he said, rummaging through the box. "This is the gold cloth Oi wore in processions." He handed it to Tong and she unfolded it. It was bigger than a tablecloth and glittered with flecks of gold thread.

After a few minutes, Ms. Sandra said it was time to go. Loong Kow asked Lily to wait a

moment.

"Bend down here," he said. Lily knelt in front of him and leaned in closer. He touched her face gently and whispered, "You have seen one."

It was a statement, not a question. How did he know? Lily did not know what to say. If she said yes, then the news might get out. Others would find out and many people would be looking for Rambu. Could she risk it? She answered with a question.

"And what happens if I say yes?"

Uncle was silent for a moment. Then he nodded his head. "Yes. I see the difficulty. Perhaps you saw one in your dream?"

Lily smiled. "Yes, it was a beautiful dream."

Loong Kow nodded, and Lily stood up. Even though he could not see her, she put her hands to her chin and bowed slightly.

"Thank you so much."

Outside, Sandra and Tong talked quietly.

"Thank you," Lily said. "It was so nice to meet you and your grandfather." She hesitated. "Can I ask you about the rings on your neck? Why do you wear them? Do they hurt?"

Tong smiled. "It is tradition for girls to wear them in my tribe. We start wearing them around age five. It's expected now," she added, a little sadly. "Many tourists come to our village to see us so we must keep wearing them. It's okay. They are part of me now." Tong gently touched the gold rings.

Lily nodded. She understood. Many people made crafts and jewelry in the villages to sell to tourists, just like her mother and sister made bead bracelets for Sandra to sell. It was necessary to make a living and to help the family.

"I hope you can visit again," Tong said. "I don't know many girls my age."

Lily nodded happily. "I would love that!" She was so excited to have a new friend – two new friends if you counted Loong Kow – in her life.

As Lily climbed on the back of Sandra's scooter, she turned and waved. Tong waved back and Lily saw a flash of light as the sun glinted off the golden rings around her neck.

When Lily arrived home, it was late afternoon. She sensed, rather than saw, that something was not quite right. First, there were two very bright and shiny red motorcycles pulled up next to the stairs of her house. Then she heard some unfamiliar voices. For some reason, she felt scared. They rarely had any visitors, especially those with brand new motorbikes. She did not know whether to stay or run and hide. What should she do?

Chapter 10

TROUBLE

Lily climbed the stairs and paused right outside the entrance to the house and listened. It was a man's voice she didn't recognize.

"And you saw this elephant?" he asked.

Lily's heart stopped. Were they talking about Rambu?

To her surprise, it was Jasmine who answered.

"Well... not exactly. But Lily, my sister, told me about it."

"Jasmine," her mother scolded. "Why are you making up stories?"

"I'm not! I swear!" Jasmine answered. "Just wait until Lily gets back. She'll tell you!"

Lily backed away from the door and tripped over a bucket on her way down the stairs. The two policemen heard the clatter and ran out to see what the noise was.

Lily reached the last step and heard one of the men and her father call after her.

"Come back here!"

Lily froze. What should she do? If she ran, they would chase her with their motorcycles. She couldn't outrun them. She turned slowly and looked toward the top of the stairs. Two policemen in army green-colored uniforms stood scowling down at her. They each had a gun holstered at a belt around their waist. Both had very short, cropped hair and caps that matched their uniforms.

"I'm sorry," she said, although she wasn't sure what she was sorry for.

"I just got back. What's wrong?" She slowly climbed back up the stairs, her heart thumping so loudly in her chest that she was sure they could see it.

"Come inside," one of the officers motioned sternly.

Lily nodded and slid past the two men, her parents, and Jasmine. Jasmine had a look of satisfaction on her face. What had she done? Inside, her mother pulled up two plastic chairs for the men to sit on. They sat on the floor in front of the men.

"We have had a report," the older one started, "that you have seen a white elephant in the forest. As you know, all white elephants belong to the king. Is this true?"

"A report?" Lily asked. "A report from who? That is crazy."

Jasmine folded her arms across her chest defiantly.

"It was me! I reported it!" she said. "You told me about the white elephant and showed me a picture of it. I went to the village and called the police."

Lily wanted to reach out and pull all of Jasmine's hair out and wipe that smug look off her face. Instead, she tried to remain calm. "It was just a picture from my imagination," she said. "Of course, I didn't see one. I just said that to get attention." She bowed her head, as if ashamed of her actions. She wondered how many incenses she would have to burn at the temple to make up for all her lying.

"She's lying!" Jasmine said. "She dropped beads in the forest on her way back so she could find the elephant again. Why would she do that if the elephant wasn't real?"

"I did drop the beads," Lily said sadly to her mom. "I'm so sorry. There was a hole in the bag from when I fell in the creek."

Jasmine glared at her. Lily had to keep herself from smiling.

"I'm sorry," Mah said to the policemen, "to make you come all this way."

The policemen rose, looking at them all sternly. "You need to watch your daughters more carefully," the younger one said. "Making up lies and wasting our time is not what the police are for."

They all put their hands to their faces in a *wai* and bowed their heads to the police.

"Of course, of course," Lily's father said, ushering them out. "We are very sorry."

As soon as the police left, her mother strode to the corner and grabbed her yardstick. "What are you two doing? Telling lies and bringing trouble on us!" she said in a low, stern voice.

Jasmine crumpled to the floor, her head in her hands, and began to sob. Lily stared at the stick.

Her mother was strict, but she had never raised a stick to them before. Her father gently leaned over and took the stick from Mah's hand.

"Mah!" he said quietly, "They are just girls... kids."

"They brought shame to us!" her mother spat back. "The police came here!"

Lily didn't hear the rest of the conversation. She ran to her room and hid under the bed. Her Mother's threats scared her, but it hurt her more that Jasmine had told her secret. Why did Jasmine hate her so? She didn't know. She only knew that she could never trust her sister with a secret again.

Chapter 11

YOU ARE ENOUGH

Lily woke up the next morning with her stomach growling. She had fallen asleep without eating after all the trouble the night before. She climbed out of bed and looked out her window. Dark gray clouds were gathering around the mountains, brightening the colors of the rice fields to a shimmering gold.

She could smell the fresh scent of the rain, like clean skin after a bath. It would soon sweep down on them like sheets of liquid silver.

She peered around the door. Her mother and Jasmine sat on the vinyl mat, silently working the colorful beads back and forth with their needles. It was as if nothing had happened. Her mother glanced up when Lily came out.

"Do your chores" her mother said. "Then there is rice and vegetables in the kitchen for you to eat."

Jasmine said nothing and did not look up. Lily went down the stairs and found the bucket of seed for the chickens. They gathered around her, clucking and pecking on the dirt where she scattered their food.

There was a small lean-to where the hens had built nests and she searched through them, collecting three freshly laid eggs. Perhaps her mother would make her an omelet with them.

She set the eggs in a tin can on the stairs and made her way toward Fatty who squealed at her. She would have to gather the green leaves from a nearby pond to feed her.

Next to Fatty was their water buffalo, *Chai Dee*, which meant "good heart." She was slowly chewing a bucket of hay. She looked at Lily with soft, soulful eyes.

Lily patted her softly in between her horns. Chai Dee had been with them a long time. During the harvest, after her father had gathered up the bundles of rice, she and Jasmine would climb up on Chai Dee and ride her around.

There was a trick to riding a water buffalo. You had to grab its tail from behind, use the curve of its back leg to step up, and pull yourself up onto its back.

Some buffalo didn't like it; they would turn their head toward the rider and try to swipe them with their horns. But Chai Dee was different. She was always patient and would walk around slowly, chewing hay and swishing her tail back and forth.

Down the hill, Lily saw her father, walking slowly through the rice fields, pausing now and then to bend down and check an emerald blade of rice.

In September, there wasn't a lot to do. In May, however, which was the planting season, she remembered how hard he worked. He had walked through the shin-high water with a wooden cart full of rice seedlings by his side. Up and down the rows he went, planting the seedlings with utmost care. There was a beautiful rhythm to it, but she knew how hard it was.

While planting, he wore only blue cotton loose pants and no shirt. The sun glistened on his thin, muscular frame. A round straw hat sat on his head. Occasionally he would stand up to stretch his back, but then the routine would start again. He did this from dawn to night until all the seedlings were planted. Sometimes Mah and Jasmine would help.

They would all groan from back pain at the end of the day from bending over so long.

Today her father looked more relaxed. The rains were plenty and that meant the rice was growing well. This was the waiting time, until, in a few months, the crop would turn a golden brown and it would be time to harvest it.

"Pah," she said quietly, coming up behind him.

He turned to her. "How are you today *dok-mai lek*?" he asked, calling her "little flower." That was his nickname for her.

Lily shrugged. "I'm ok," she said.

He nodded. "Get your chores done?"

"Yes, I am getting them done."

"Good," he said, turning back to inspect the rice stalks.

The water was up to Lily's shins as she padded through behind him. An occasional crab stuck his pincers up above the muddy water as they walked. "I'm sorry," she said to his back.

"I know," he said, without breaking his movements. He turned then, looking down at her. "You must understand. It is a hard life we lead. Your mother works hard. Her reputation means a lot to her."

"I know. But…"

He raised his thin brows, eyes twinkling. "Yes?" he encouraged her.

"She doesn't love me," she said softly. "She thinks I'm broken."

He stopped and reached out a hand to touch her shoulder. "She loves you. She isn't sure how to show her love sometimes. Life has… disappointed her."

"What do you mean?"

Her father hesitated. "She didn't expect to be a farmer's wife, to live here in the mountains. But it was all I knew.

Then her Mah died when she was only sixteen. She had to grow up fast. Right after we married, my father died and left me this land. So, we had to stay. Your mother wanted to live in a big city, like Chiang Mai, and have a business. So, this was a disappointment to her."

Lily thought about his words. It was hard to imagine her mother and father being young and having dreams of another kind of life. But she could understand it. How many times had she dreamt of living in another country and having adventures?

"You don't seem disappointed," she said.

He motioned around him. "I am content. I look around here at all the beauty, at you, at my family, and it is enough for me. You," he emphasized, "are enough."

She hugged his waist then, and they stood like that for a minute. How different he and her mother were.

She knew they had different beliefs.

Her father had attended a Catholic school when he was young. He didn't talk about it much, but she had seen the worn bible and rosary he had next to his bed.

Mah was a devout Buddhist and gave incense and food to the Buddha in the wat or temple to keep the dark spirits away. Mah also put food and incense in their own spirit house, which was a temple the size of a dollhouse, that almost every Thai home had in their yard.

Lily wasn't sure what she believed. She was faithful to go to the temple with her mother, but occasionally she visited a local church in a nearby village with her dad. He didn't go often, however, because her mother did not approve.

"Go on now," he said, "and finish your chores. And be patient with your mother."

Lily turned back up the hill toward the house. As she did, big drops of rain began to pelt her skin. It didn't matter. Her father would continue to walk the fields, she would continue to gather greens for Fatty, and Jasmine and her mother would continue to work on the bracelets, pausing only to change the station on the radio to listen to their favorite show or music. This was her life, she thought. Everything was the same. And yet, everything felt different, like the colors around her were brighter, and the hole she carried around inside her was a little less empty today. That feeling had a name, and it was Rambu.

Chapter 12

DISCOVERED

The next day, Lily's mother sent her to Sandra again for more beads and to take the completed bracelets to her. Right after, Lily intended to find Rambu. She had several bananas in her bag for him. It was almost time for their school to start up again and this worried her. What if she had less time to visit with Rambu?

After seeing Ms. Sandra, Lily said goodbye and ran toward the edge of the village, passed the mango tree and stream until she reached The Golden Rain Tree. But Rambu wasn't there. She waited as long as she could, waving the bananas from her bag in the air.

"Where are you Rambu?" she asked out

loud.

It was getting late, and her mother would be upset if she didn't get home soon. She turned to go, leaving the bananas behind her. She would have to come back one more time and try to see him. She ran back toward the village. As she came out of the forest, she saw Lek and the other boys playing soccer. Could she sneak past them without them seeing her? She moved to her left toward the trail up to her house, but as she did, the soccer ball flew directly at her. It bounced off her shoulder and disappeared into the forest. She grabbed her shoulder, trying not to cry from the pain. The boys all laughed at her.

Suddenly, from the forest, the soccer ball came flying back out. The boys' eyes grew wide, and they stared into the darkness. One of them pointed.

"Ghost!" he yelled. "There's a ghost in

there."

As if to confirm their cries, a loud "honk" echoed out of the forest.

"Rambu!" Lily whispered. "Oh no!"

Rambu had kicked the soccer ball back to them. If Rambu came to the village, everyone would know about him. He would be taken away! Before she could stop him, his pink trunk and speckled ears peered out of the forest. Then he stepped out, looking around, searching with his trunk. He walked directly to Lily, sniffing at her bag.

"Rambu!" she said. "No! Come on! Let's go!" She held out a banana to him, trying to lead him back into the forest. But Lek and his friends stood in their way. They stared at Rambu. One of them reached out to touch his ear.

"Is that… a white elephant?" one of them asked in awe.

"It is, isn't it?" Lek asked Lily. "Where did you find him?"

Lily shook her head. "No. It's just a plain old elephant." She had to get Rambu away.

Lek shook his head. "Look. He's practically pink here, his eyes are light… If he's a white elephant, he must go to the king. We could get a lot of money for him!"

"No!" Lily cried suddenly, losing all fear of the boys. "He's NOT for sale! To anyone!"

Lek shoved her away. "Not if we have anything to say about it!" He turned to one of the boys. "Go get a rope so we can tie him up. Then we'll call the police!"

"Come on Rambu!" Lily called. "Let's go!" She walked toward the forest, holding out a banana. Rambu began to follow her. One of the boys handed Lek a rope, who threw it around Rambu's head and pulled it tight. Rambu shook his head back and forth.

"Get away!" Lily cried, trying to push Lek away. But he was too big.

Rambu stopped suddenly, pawing at the dirt. He refused to budge. Lek was pulling one way, and Lily was trying to drag him toward the cover of the forest. Suddenly, Lek dropped the rope, staring at the ground.

"What… what is that?" Lek asked.

Lily followed where his arm was pointing. Rambu had picked up a small stick and was making scratches in the dirt. Lily stared in disbelief. Rambu had written out: L–I–L-Y in crooked Thai letters. He had written her name. And beside it, he scrawled out the Thai word *puen* which meant "friend," as if to say "Lily is my friend."

Lek's eyes grew wide, and he backed away. "Are you… using magic?" he asked Lily.

"No!" Lily cried. "Of course, I'm not!"

Rambu honked again. Suddenly, from just

beyond the edge of the forest, a thunderous roar rang out along with the crashing of tree limbs. The boys turned and ran as Rambu's mother burst through the trees, running toward them, her giant ears flapping. Lily was frozen standing next to Rambu. His mother stopped suddenly and turned toward Rambu, wrapping a long trunk around his side and pulling him to her. She guided him back into the safety of the dark trees.

Lily realized she had been holding her breath from fear. She let out a big sigh. The boys had disappeared. She was standing alone, shaking. What would they do? They would tell their parents about Rambu, she was sure. There would be police and others searching for Rambu now, to take him away from here.

"What have I done?" she asked herself. How was she ever going to keep Rambu safe now?

Chapter 13

A CALL FOR HELP

Lily burst into the Rainbow House, breathing heavily. Sandra, who had been placing bracelets into a box to mail, looked up, concern on her face.

"Lily! What's wrong?"

"I… I need Loong Kow! I need his help!"

Sandra led Lily to a pink plastic chair, urging her to sit. *"Pen rai?"* she asked. What's wrong?

Lily took a deep breath and looked around to see if anyone was nearby. Three ladies from the village were sitting away from them. She decided to confide in Ms. Sandra, and she lowered her voice.

"Ms. Sandra," she said in a whisper, "I have a *puen*," she said, using the word for *friend* that Rambu had just scratched in the dirt. "It is a *chang kow*," Lily said saying white elephant in Thai. She paused and searched Ms. Sandra's face to see if she believed her.

Ms. Sandra smiled. "This is good, no?"

Lily shook her head, brushing away a tear. She switched to her broken English. "No! People… boys… see him. They see Rambu! They come take him away!" Lily buried her head in her hands. Great sobs came from her. Sandra placed a tender hand on her head. "Please…" Lily said, through her tears. "Can you tell Loong Kow? I need his help. Can you take him a letter?'

Sandra nodded. "Of course!"

Lily grabbed a piece of paper and a pencil and wrapped her two fingers around the pencil like she had been practicing with the paint-brush. She had to go slow, but she realized she could form the words better now since she had been painting.

"My elephant is in trouble," she wrote. "Can you come help?" Then she handed it to Sandra. *"Kawp kuhn*, Ms. Sandra," she said. "Thank you."

"Wait a minute," Ms. Sandra said, motion-ing for Lily to follow her.

She lead her outside and down a set of ce-ment stairs to the left of the entrance. It was dark, but Ms. Sandra flicked a switch and a bare bulb came on. Dim light spread over the room. It was a storeroom with boxes piled high, large paint cans, and several kinds of tools.

"Take this," Sandra said. She leaned down and selected a can of paint and a paintbrush. "It is gray. For now, until we have a better idea, you should paint your friend with this." Sandra made a sweeping motion with the paintbrush so Lily would understand. "That way, if someone goes searching for him, they won't notice him right away."

Lily was flooded with relief. What a great idea! Surely this would work, at least for a while. She put her hands together and bowed her head over her hands in a deep and grateful *wai.* "Thank you so much, Ms. Sandra." She hugged Ms. Sandra around the waist, grabbed the paint, and ran up the stairs. She must hurry. She must paint Rambu and then quickly return home. She knew she would be in trouble. It was already late. But it didn't matter. Nothing mattered except saving Rambu.

Chapter 14

THE NEW GRAY ELEPHANT

It took her an hour to find Rambu. She called for him over and over. Finally, his pink-speckled trunk poked through the brush. He had another present for her. It was a stick of sugar cane. She kissed him on his trunk.

"Thank you Rambu. But I'm not here to play."

She quickly undid the paint can and dipped the brush in the gray paint. She lathered the color onto his trunk, ears, and the rest of his body. She paused to remove a few spots from her shirt, and Rambu grabbed the paintbrush and waved it up in the air. Dark droplets spilled out on his back and dripped down his sides. She laughed.

"No Rambu! It's not time to play. I've got to protect you."

Finally, she was done. She stepped back to analyze her work. It would do for now. From head to toe, Rambu was completely gray. Unfortunately, his eyes showed a lovely color of pink, and his eyelashes were like pale gold feathers. But there was nothing she could do about it.

She gave him her last banana and turned to go. He reached out his trunk and tapped her back. She turned toward him. He reached up and gathered a stalk of the yellow buds from the tree above her and handed them to her.

"Oh Rambu! I love you so much. I hope nothing bad will happen to you." She kissed the tip of his trunk, hid the paint can and brush in the crook of a nearby tree, and ran home. It was almost dark. Her mother would be furious.

She arrived home just as the sun was setting. She began to climb the stairs but then saw her father, mother, and Jasmine behind the house looking at something. She went towards them and saw, just beyond them, a large gray figure lying on the ground. It was their water buffalo, Good Heart.

"What happened?" she asked, looking at the still figure in front of them.

Jasmine glared at her. "What do you care?" she smirked. "You're never here anyway."

Her father put a hand on Jasmine's shoulder.

"It's no one's fault," he said. "It was her time to go."

"No, no!" Lily cried. "What about the harvest, Pah? You need a buffalo to harvest the rice."

Pah shook his head sadly. "I don't know, little flower."

Mah shook her head, her lips set firmly together. It was her angry face. But she said nothing. There was nothing to say. Somehow, by working harder and selling more bracelets, they would have to find the money to get a new buffalo. Lily knew that a buffalo costs thousands of baht. It would take half a year's salary. What could they do?

She knelt beside Chai Dee, stroking the smooth, black part of her nose and touching the yellowed horns that curve up like the letter Y around her head. She looked like she was sleeping, her dark brown eyes closed now to the world.

That night, Lily heard her parents arguing. She knew what it was about. How were they to raise that much money before harvest time? Should they make a loan and go into debt?

Lily took her cedar box from its hiding place and opened it up. Here were all her most prized treasures from Rambu. The blue ribbon, the shiny purple stone… Suddenly she had an idea. She picked up the clam and opened it up, admiring the shiny white stone. Maybe, she thought, maybe she could help her family after all.

Chapter 15

THE PEARL

The next day, after Lily finished her chores, she took the pearl from the cedar box and ran down to the village. Lek and his friends were playing soccer again. At first, a few boys teased her, calling her "two fingers" and "scary witch." But this time, Lek raised a hand and turned to the other boys, and told them to stop. Then, he stepped aside slightly for Lily to go by. She couldn't believe it. Somehow, what happened the day before with Rambu had changed Lek's mind about her. She didn't understand it, but she was grateful. She was glad she had stood up to him. Thank you, Rambu, she whispered to herself.

Ms. Sandra was going through a box of colored beads when Lily arrived. "All is good?" she asked.

Lily nodded. "Yes. Thank you. Help me please again?"

Lily turned her back so no one else could see and opened the brown clam. When the perfectly round, pale gem was revealed, Ms. Sandra gasped.

"Lily!" she said. "Where did you get this?"

"Rambu!" she whispered. "He brings me—" she paused, trying to think of the word in English. "Like what you get for birthday?"

Sandra understood. "Presents?"

Lily nodded. "Yes. Presents."

Sandra rubbed a finger over the pearl lovingly. Lily wasn't sure Ms. Sandra believed her.

"I no steal!" she said firmly. "I no lie." She paused. "I no lie a lot!" she corrected.

Ms. Sandra smiled.

"Can you help again? Take this to store in big town? Get money? Our *kwai*… it died. Pah need a new *kwai*." She couldn't remember the English word, buffalo, for *kwai*. But Ms. Sandra understood.

"I'm so sorry," Ms. Sandra said. "Of course! Let me see what I can do."

Lily gave her the clam and pearl and thanked Ms. Sandra again. She wanted to go see Rambu but when she stepped outside, she saw five policemen talking to Lek and his friends. *Oh no! They already told them about Rambu!* She quickly hid in a narrow alley between two buildings. If they saw her, they would recognize her and ask her questions.

Lily peered out from behind the cement wall. One of the boys, she didn't know his name, pointed toward the fore! He was telling the police about Rambu! What could she do?

There was nothing. She would just have to trust that the gray paint would hide Rambu's true color.

The policemen took off into the forest, spreading out to cover more area. One of them had a walkie-talkie and spoke into it. The others responded. She could hear the crackle of the other walkie-talkies.

Lily shook all over. She did not know what to do! She wanted to cry and scream at the same time. Lily didn't know how long she waited there, hiding in between the two buildings. She slid down, hugging her knees, trying to keep from crying. She heard Ms. Sandra's scooter and peeked out. Was she going to get Loong Kow? Lily prayed she was.

Her legs began to cramp up. She didn't know how long she sat like that. Finally, she peeked out again. To her surprise, the villagers crowded together in the middle of the street.

She was close enough to hear them murmuring the words "white elephant" and "searching for." Her heart sank.

A few minutes later, there was a cheer from the crowd. Lily stepped out to see what was happening. One of the policemen had a rope around Rambu's head and was urging Rambu on by dangling a banana in front of him. Fortunately, Rambu's gray paint still covered most of his body. Some of the crowd was examining Rambu, touching his sides and ears.

"He's not white," one villager exclaimed. Lily sighed with relief. Would the gray paint fool them?

"It was the only baby elephant we found," said the policeman.

"His eyes are strange," another villager said. "Is he blind?" he asked, referring to the strange, faded color of Rambu's eyes.

Lily slowly stepped out into the road, peering around the people who had gathered to examine Rambu. She didn't want to get too close. If Rambu saw her he might try and come to her.

"We must have an expert from the King's palace examine him," the policemen said.

"Oh no!" Lily thought. *Were they taking him away?*

And then, the worst possible thing happened.

Chapter 16

TRUE COLORS

It began to rain. Just a sprinkle at first, but then it started to pick up, turning into a steady drip.

Someone said, "Look," and some of the villagers pointed at Rambu. "The gray is washing off. It has a light color underneath."

That was it, Lily said to herself. It was all over. Now they would see Rambu's true color. So be it. If this was the last time she would see him, then she would get close to him and say goodbye.

She pushed her way through the crowd. At first, it was difficult, but suddenly, behind her, the crowd parted. To Lily's amazement, there stood Loong Kow and Tong. Loong Kow had a walking stick, and Tong held his arm, ushering him forward slowly. The rings around Tong emphasized her long, graceful neck and she held her head high as she ushered Loong Kow forward. She heard the villagers gasp and whisper.

"She's from the Kayan Tribe!"

"I've never seen the long necks before."

It occurred to Lily that anyone different was often talked about.

Some of the policemen seemed to know Loong Kow. They all greeted him with a *wai*. Tong whispered something to her grandfather and the old man nodded his head.

"Loong Kow," the older policeman said, "it's good you are here. We have found a white elephant to take to the king."

Loong Kow reached his hand out toward the elephant. Rambu's trunk curled up toward his face and Loong Kow smiled. Then, as if sensing Lily's presence, he reached out and touched Lily's arm. Lily smiled despite the tears flowing down her cheeks.

"Are you sure?" Loong Kow asked quietly. "That it is a white elephant? You would not want to embarrass your village if you are wrong."

The older policeman frowned. "It has all the markings, Loong," he said.

Loong Kow pet Rambu on the head. "I see. All seven characteristics of a white elephant?" he asked.

The policeman hesitated. "Seven?"

"Are his eyes white?" he asked.

The policeman examined Rambu's pale eyes. "Yes," he said firmly.

"And in his mouth, does he have a white soft palate?"

The policeman held out a banana to Rambu so Rambu would open his mouth. The police-man glanced inside Rambu's mouth. "Yes!" he said excitedly. "It's kind of pale pink."

Loong Kow nodded. There was a growing

excitement in the crowd. How famous their village would be if they had a sacred white elephant! Lily's heart sank. What was Loong Kow doing? Didn't he know they would take Rambu away?

Loong Kow calmly continued. "And white hair? And a white tail?" he asked.

The policeman brushed away what was left of the gray paint to reveal the pinkish-white skin. "Yes!" he said excitedly.

What was happening? Loong Kow was about to pronounce Rambu a white elephant. She met Tong's eyes. Tong smiled reassuringly. She did not seem to be worried.

"Hmm," Loong Kow said. "Maybe…" Then he stopped and put a bony finger in the air. "Ah!" he said. "One last sign and this is the most important. White elephants, because they are sacred, will never follow another human on their own, unless you have food he likes. They only follow other white elephants. They are holy! Set apart from humans. So… let's try an experiment. Tong," he said, "walk away and see if Rambu will follow you."

Tong obeyed and began to walk away. Rambu stood still. The crowd murmured excitedly. Loong Kow chose another young boy and told him to walk away, but still Rambu didn't follow. The villagers began to clap. Finally, Loong Kow reached out and touched Lily's shoulder.

"One more volunteer," he said. Lily knew he meant her.

"Let me please," she said. She began to slowly walk away from Rambu. She had to force herself not to look back. *Please, Rambu. Please follow me.*

At first, there was no movement, and the crowd murmured excitedly among themselves. But then, she heard the crowd gasp in surprise and disappointment. She stopped, smiling. Lily felt Rambu's soft trunk sniffing her hair, moving down her back, curling around her waist, and pulling her to him. She turned around and wrapped her arms around his neck. "Good boy, Rambu" she whispered. "Good boy."

"I'm afraid it is not a true white elephant," Lung Kow said. "I am very sorry."

The policeman nodded, disappointment on his face. "Thank you, Loong Kow. You have saved us all from embarrassment."

Loong Kow bowed slightly to the man. Around them, the crowd began to disperse. There was nothing more to see here.

In the distance, she saw Lek standing with his hands crossed against his chest, glaring in Lily's direction. Lek knew, she thought. He knew her secret.

Chapter 17

SAFE FOR NOW

Loong Kow and Tong walked with Lily and Rambu toward the edge of the forest.

"I think it's time for Rambu to go home now," Loong said.

Lily nodded. "Thank you so much," Lily said, "to both of you."

"And Lily," he added, "we saved Rambu this time. He must not be easy to find again. Do you understand?"

She nodded sadly. "Yes." She knew what he meant. The older Rambu got, the more his "whiteness" would increase. If Lily kept visiting him, he might come to the village more often. She knew she could not take that risk. "But it's so hard to let him go!"

Loong Kow nodded. "I know. But sometimes what is best for those we care about is not always best for us." He added, "Rambu is a baby now and needs his mother. But when he gets older, he MUST go to the king. But it will be a good life for him. He will be treated very well and be famous. Okay?"

Again, Lily nodded. "Thank you," she said again.

Lily walked into the forest and Rambu followed her. They passed the mango tree and Lily picked up a yellow mango off the ground, peeled it with her fingers, and fed pieces of it to Rambu as they walked. He transferred the golden, sweet meat into his mouth as quickly as she handed it to him. He was always hungry!

After walking past the creek, which bubbled

happily, they found their way to the Golden Rain Tree. In the distance, she heard Rambu's mother calling out to him. Rambu lifted his trunk in the air and responded with a similar honk.

"Time for you to go see your mother," Lily said. "And me too."

Rambu once again reached above her and grasped a handful of the lemon-colored flowers and gave them to her. She took them and kissed him on his head. He turned and left, back through the thick brush of the forest. She wondered, sadly, if she would ever see him again.

Brushing tears from her eyes, she left the forest and climbed the path that led up the mountain and to her house. The sun was low in the sky, and it reminded her of the golden mango that she had fed to Rambu.

She climbed the steps up to her house and

was surprised to see Ms. Sandra sitting there on the vinyl mat next to her mother and father. They were all drinking sweet tea.

"Come sit!" her mother motioned to Lily. She hoped she wasn't in trouble again, but her mother wore a genuine smile on her face.

Lily handed the bouquet of golden flowers to Sandra. "A present for you," she said in English. Sandra smelled the bouquet and smiled. Sandra had done so much for her, Lily thought. How could she ever thank her?

"Thank you," Sandra said. "Maybe you could translate for us?" Lily nodded. "First of all, tell your mother that you have been a big help to me at The Rainbow Store."

Lily stared at Ms. Sandra. "I'm sorry," she said. "My mother not like me talk about me."

Ms. Sandra nodded, understanding. "Okay." She reached over and put a hand on Lily's knee and said, "Lily *kohn dee mak*!" which meant, "Lily is a good person!" She couldn't believe Ms. Sandra was complimenting her in front of her parents. She heard Jasmine, who was behind the wall listening, utter something like "humph." Lily's mother raised her eyebrows in surprise, but both her parents said thank you.

Sandra slid a hand into the pocket of her skirt and brought out a white envelope. "Rainbow House has been doing really well this year thanks to all of you who are working so hard." She paused and Lily did her best to translate. "Because of this," Sandra went on, "there is extra money for the workers. And this is your share." Sandra smiled at Lily and handed the envelope to her mother. Her mother's eyes widened as she looked through the envelope.

Lily's mother looked at Lily with a confused look. "What is this for?" she asked in Thai.

"It's okay, Mah," Lily assured her. "It's extra money from Rainbow House. We can use it to buy another buffalo for the harvest!"

To Lily's surprise, a tear streamed down her mother's face.

Pah looked at Lily. "Are you sure, Lily?" he asked. "Was this something you did?"

Lily shook her head. "No, Pah. It's nothing I did." She couldn't tell him the truth. That it was something magical that Rambu did. She knew now that Sandra had sold the pearl and that this was the money.

They all talked for a few more minutes and then Sandra rose to go. Lily walked out with her.

"Thank you, Ms. Sandra," Lily said. "Thank you so much!"

"You did it!" Ms. Sandra said, placing a hand on Lily's shoulder. "You are brave and kind! You helped Rambu!"

Lily did not understand the word brave, but she saw the happiness on Ms. Sandra's face and understood. "I think," she said, "that Rambu help me."

After Ms. Sandra left, she went into her room and pulled out the cedar box with the presents that Rambu had given her.

"So, you're the hero now!"

Lily turned to see Jasmine standing behind her. She had her arms crossed against her chest and her eyes narrowed in anger.

"Jasmine," Lily said softly, "why do you hate me so much?"

The question took her sister by surprise. "I… I don't hate you. I just don't like you all the time. You get away with everything. You never get in trouble. You don't have to work because of your stupid hand!"

"Don't you think I would trade it all to be like you?" Lily asked. "You have everything.

Mah loves you more because you aren't broken, and you are beautiful." Lily's voice caught in her throat. She didn't want to cry in front of Jasmine.

Jasmine plopped down on Lily's bed. "I didn't know that," she said quietly. "I didn't know you felt that way."

They were both quiet for a moment, feeling awkward about sharing their feelings. They had never done that before.

"I heard about the elephant," Jasmine said. Lily nodded. "I'm sorry, that he's not a magical white elephant."

Lily smiled. "It's okay. He's magical to me."

Jasmine stood up. "I've got to get back to work now."

"Wait," Lily said. She rummaged in her cedar box and brought out the blue silk ribbon and the purple stone that Rambu had given her.

"I wanted to give these to you."

Jasmine examined the silky ribbon and the rough texture of the stone. "Thank you," she said, smiling. "They are lovely. Why are you giving them to me?"

"Let's just say it's a start to being better friends and sisters."

Jasmine thought a moment and then nodded. "Okay. It's a deal."

reached up to snatch the yellow flowers from the tree and handed them to her.

"That's not fair," she said. "You are bribing me." He shook his head again. "My dear friend, you have changed my life and I will always be grateful. You will be in my heart forever." Tears streamed down her face, and Rambu gently snuffled her cheeks with his trunk as if wiping away her tears. His pale, pink eyes looked sad, and she wondered if elephants cried. "Go now. Go see your mom." Rambu shook his head. "You must go, Rambu. You must go and not come back here." She took a banana and lead him to the edge of the brush where he usually passed through. He picked up a stick off the ground and etched in the dirt: "L-I-L-Y Fren."

"I will always be your friend, Rambu. Thank you."

He snatched the banana from her and with

one last look at Lily, he disappeared into the thick, lush branches.

Lily turned and ran, but she couldn't outrun the deep sobs that burst forth with every step. She ran harder as if trying to escape the sadness that overwhelmed her.

She burst out of the forest and as if echoing her tears, drops of rain began to pelt her, soaking the white shirt and navy skirt of her school uniform. She kept running, up the path to her house, passed the bridge and the pond of pink lilies until she stumbled up the steps into their house. Her mother, who was making curry paste in a mortar and pestle, looked up, startled by her sudden appearance.

"Lily! What's wrong?"

Lily couldn't speak. She squatted down, her head in her hands, cradling her two-fingered hand. Her mother came to her, saying nothing, only wrapping her arms around her until Lily's sobs subsided.

"Was it the boys?" her mother asked. "Did they tease you again?"

Lily shook her head. "No. I'm not afraid of them anymore."

"Then what?"

Lily lifted her head and looked into her mother's sympathetic eyes. "Have you ever lost a good friend?" she asked.

Mah smiled. "Yes. When I was your age."

"And did it feel... like this? Like your heart would break?"

Mah nodded. "Yes. But she – my friend – still lives here with me. In my heart. What happened to your friend?"

"My friend had to leave and go live some-where else," Lily said. "What about yours?"

"My friend... was a silly puppy," she said, embarrassed. "His name was Pepsi! He was black and he loved to drink Pepsi!"

Lily found herself giggling. "I didn't know that."

"I never told you," Mah said. "I thought it would make me seem silly and weak. But I think you needed to hear it today. I loved that dog. We went everywhere together. Once I fell in the rice fields and hurt my ankle. He ran back and brought my father to help me. I had him for ten years. And one day, he tried to fight a snake and got bit. I held him in my arms until his last breath." Lily was surprised to see tears on her mother's cheeks. "When you love," she added, "there is happiness but also pain. You cannot have love without it."

That night, Lily went to her desk and looked at all the paintings she and Rambu had done together. Rambu liked the bright blue, red, and purple streaks. Lily's had green rice fields, gray mountains, and, in the middle, their small brown house on stilts.

She glanced out her window. It was getting dark, but she could see the outline of rain clouds billowing up and preparing for rain. She heard frogs, each one with a different tone. It reminded her of the monks chanting in the temples. She felt happy that at last she had been able to help her parents, even if they didn't know about it. And Rambu was safe from being taken away, at least for now, thanks to Loong Kow and Tong. But she knew she had done the right thing. It was too dangerous for him to be so close to the village. And Mah's story helped her to know that sometimes loving another was difficult. She understood Mah a little more now. And Jasmine… well, it was a start.

Lily closed the cedar box and put her paintings away. She had school tomorrow. In the past she had always dreaded it, being teased about her two-fingered hand. But she had a feeling that at least the boys in the village wouldn't be quite so brave anymore. She giggled to herself, remembering the frightened look on Lek's face when Rambu wrote in the dirt.

In the distance, she heard the call of a grown elephant, followed by a fainter honk that she knew was Rambu and his mother. Perhaps they were telling her goodbye.

She remembered Rambu's lovely writing. *Fren. Lily is my fren.*

Yes, she thought. *And you, my dear Rambu, will always be mine.*

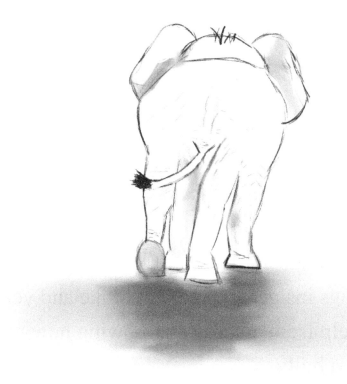

THE END

Author's Notes

<u>Bullying</u>

Are you or someone you know being bullied for looking or acting different like Lily? If so, you should know that it is not your or their fault. Also, you should tell someone, like your teacher or counselor at school. Don't keep the bad feelings inside. You are not alone and you can get help from an adult in knowing how to deal with a bully.

<u>Thai Elephants Are Endangered</u>

The Asian elephant is endangered. There are only about 3,000-4,000 left in Thailand. Many are not treated well and are forced to do "tricks" for tourists. However, many elephant sanctuaries in Thailand take very good care of elephants and allow you to visit them.

<u>Are White Elephants Real?</u>

Yes, they are real. Currently, there are about eleven white elephants belonging to the Thai king.

<u>Elephants Are Not for Riding</u>

While Lily in this story does sit on top of Rambu for a few minutes while they play in the water, many elephant sanctuaries no longer allow tourists to ride them because it can create stress for the elephant.

<u>Can Elephants Really Paint?</u>

Yes, elephants can really paint. However, it is important that they are not forced to paint if they do not want to.

I hope you enjoyed this book. Please consider writing a review to help others enjoy UNDER THE GOLDEN RAIN TREE.
Thank you!

Want to know more about Eileen Hobbs? Visit her website and follow her on social media!

https://www.eileenhobbsauthor.com

www.facebook.com/Eileenhobbsauthor
www.instagram.com/eileenhobbsauthor/

<u>**Other Books by Eileen Hobbs**</u>:

The Heath Cousins and the Moonstone Cave
The Heath Cousins and the Kingsgate Bridge
The Heath Cousins and the Crystal Canyon
The Heath Cousins and the Ruby Lantern
The Heath Cousins and the Silver Statue

About the Author

Eileen Hobbs lives in Oklahoma with her husband and two dogs. She teaches English composition to international students and Developmental Reading at a nearby university. Eileen enjoys traveling, gardening, being at the beach, and spending time with her family. She's not a typical Okie though. Eileen grew up in Thailand, where her parents were missionaries. She desires to write books that have diverse characters and that take her readers to fictional places they might not otherwise get to explore in real life. Other books by Eileen include The Heath Cousins series which are based on the growing up years of her children and their cousins.

Made in the USA
Middletown, DE
29 January 2024

48166826R00089